NANOOK & PRYCE

GONE FISHING

By Ned Crowley Pictures by Larry Day

HARPER

An Imprint of HarperCollinsPublishers

Nanook & Pryce: Gone Fishing

Text copyright © 2009 by Ned Crowley

Illustrations copyright © 2009 by Larry Day

Manufactured in China.

Library of Congress Cataloging-in-Publication Data

Day, Larry.

Nanook & Pryce : gone fishing / by Ned Crowley ; pictures by Larry Day. — 1st ed.

p.   cm.

Parka-clad friends Nanook and Pryce and their dog, Yukon, encounter many different
types of ocean life and adventure on an unexpected voyage.

ISBN 978-0-06-133641-6 (trade bdg.)

[1. Stories in rhyme.   2. Marine animals—Fiction.   3. Voyages and travels—
Fiction.   4. Adventures and adventurers—Fiction.   5. Friendship—Fiction.]   I. Crowley,
Ned.   II. Title.   III. Title: Nanook and Pryce.

PZ8.3.D3315Nan   2009   2008032095

[E]—dc22   CIP

                                                                                   AC

Typography by Jeanne L. Hogle

09   10   11   12   13   SCP   10   9   8   7   6   5   4   3   2   1

❖

First Edition

To Max and Ollie
—L.D.

To Shea, Robyn, and Grace
—N.C.

Hi, Nanook
Morning, Pryce

Baiting hooks
Drilling ice

Tangled line

Out to sea

Breakfast break
Puffins pass

Round and round   Warning barks

Fearless hound
Scaredy sharks

Trouble brewing

Creaky mast

Net ungluing   Free at last

Dolphins leap

Suntan lotion

Creeping fog
Polar breeze

Chilly dog
Fishermen freeze

Tummies growl   Pile of fish

Greedy fowl
Empty dish

Final look

Home sweet ice

Good night, Nanook.

Good night, Pryce